Written by Helen Exley and Illustrated by June Massey

Me
and my
Teacher

When I first arrived at this school, the whole class was sometimes naughty ...especially me. But our teacher didn't seem to get hassled.

She was calm and quiet,
and her rules were fair.

At first I hated school.

I felt sad and lonely.

So each day I never wanted to go in.

But my teacher has really become my friend. I discovered that she cares about the same sort of things as I do, like nature, and my Africa project.

She loves wildlife just like me, and she makes everything extra interesting.

She is so patient with me. When I proudly showed everyone the work I had done on my project, I knew she was watching, smiling.

Poor teacher!

She works so hard. Most days
she is still at school working,
long after we've all gone home to play.

I feel so sorry for her!

My teacher makes up fun things
for us all to do. When we have a race
she claps and gets a bit wild and noisy.

Sometimes she's really silly
and does silly things.
That make us very happy.

When I used to get $^0/_{10}$ my teacher waited quietly. "Keep at it", she would say with a smile.

One day I suddenly understood decimal points. "Eureka", we both said, and I think she was even happier than I was.

I love school now.

I love all the projects

and finding out about things.

The school, my friends

and my teacher

have changed me

and made feel happy and strong.

I began to notice that it's
not just me she helps.

My teacher watches out

for the sad ones and the silly ones

— and even the naughty ones.

At the end of the year

I got my very first prize.

My teacher was so pleased. She clapped

and clapped and clapped.

Suddenly the school year is over. It's time to say goodbye and to thank my teacher. But how can I ever, ever thank her?

Some of the kids may forget our teacher.

But not me —

I'll never forget her.

I think I'll hear her saying,

"Go on, stick at it" for the rest of my life.

WHAT IS A HELEN EXLEY GIFTBOOK?

Helen Exley Giftbooks cover the most powerful of all human relationships:
the bonds within families and between friends, and the theme of personal values.
No expense is spared in making sure that each book is as meaningful
a gift as it is possible to create: good to give, good to receive.
You have the result in your hands. If you have loved it – tell others!
There is no power on earth like the word-of-mouth recommendation of friends!

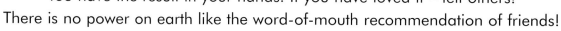

a gift for us to share

to: *Jaiden*

from: *Love* *Auntie KaKa*

2013

OTHER HELEN EXLEY GIFTBOOKS IN THIS SERIES:

Me and my Mum

Me and my Mom

Me and my Dad

Me and my Friend

Me and my Grandma

Me and my Grandpa

OTHER HELEN EXLEY GIFTBOOKS:

Giggles: A Joke Book

Crazy Kids' Jokes

To a very special Teacher

Published in 2006 by Helen Exley Giftbooks in Great Britain,
and Helen Exley Giftbooks LLC in the USA.

12 11 10 9 8 7 6 5 4 3 2 1

Illustrations © Jane Massey 2006
Copyright © Helen Exley 2006
The moral right of the author has been asserted.

ISBN 1-905130-87-2

A copy of the CIP data is available from the British Library on request.

Printed in China

Helen Exley Giftbooks, 16 Chalk Hill, Watford, Herts WD19 4BG, UK,
Helen Exley Giftbooks LLC, 185 Main Street, Spencer MA 01562, USA.
www.helenexleygiftbooks.com